Quest-terrestrials

Vol.1

Malgosia Krol
(author + illustrator)

For Elarose.

Thank you for making my world smaller yet
so much bigger than I could ever imagine possible.

When visiting other planets,
Quest-terrestrials have
ways of blending in.

But they prefer to be in the **spotlight!**

And stand out in their own unique ways...

Q-Ts like things that go fast!

Things that go faster!

And things that, um,  float?

When someone needs help,
Q-Ts do their best
            not to let each other down.

POP!

Except when they literally
need a hand getting down.

And when
someone is
feeling scared
and alone

they bring a little **light**

into the darkness.

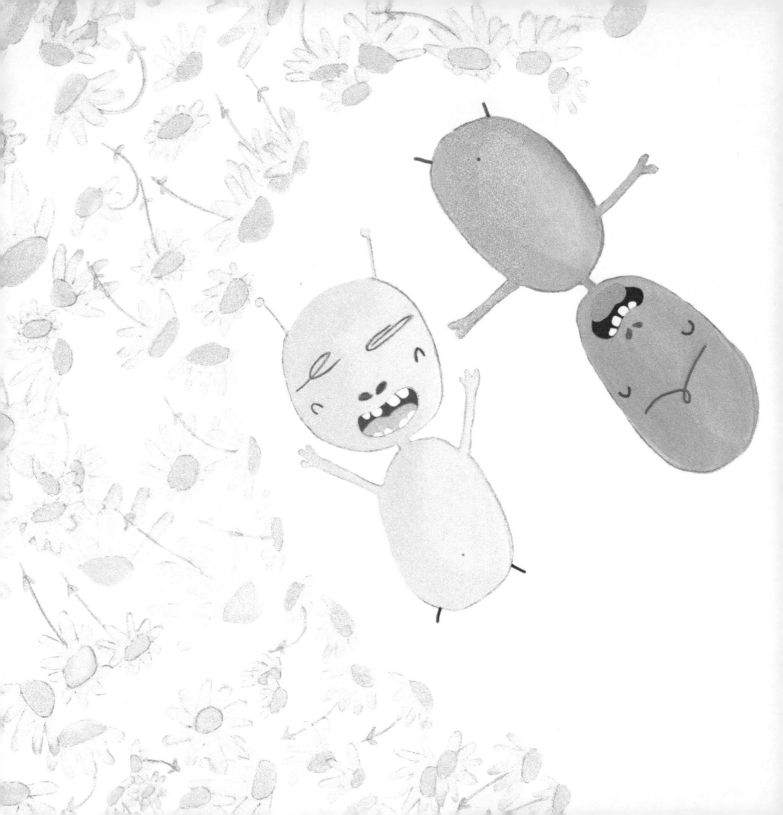

Q-Ts stop to enjoy the simple...

...and sweet things.

And love every creature that's

HAIRY!

But Q-Ts can't help going
ga-ga over some

a little more than others.

Because on their planet they

only ~~have~~ had dragons.

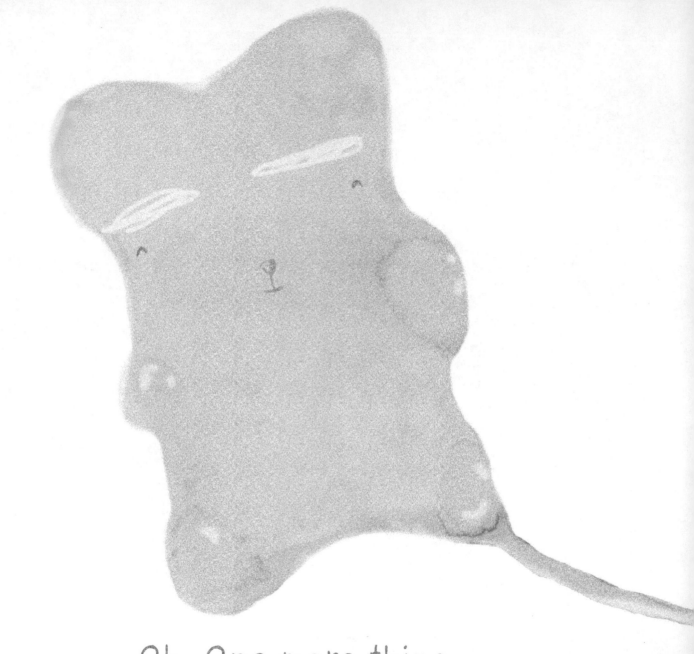

Oh. One more thing.
Their farts smell like gummy bears.

Which is **weird**,
since Q-Ts mostly eat **humans**.

Just kidding.

Acknowledgements:

A big thank you to my love, James, and his dad Beaton MacKenzie for pulling the book across the funded finish line with their generosity. And an enormous shout-out to the amazing Kickstarter supporters and all the cheerleaders for believing in this book. I feel very humbled and forever grateful.

◆ FriesenPress

Suite 300 - 990 Fort St
Victoria, BC, V8V 3K2
Canada

www.friesenpress.com

ISBN
978-1-5255-2190-4 (Hardcover)
978-1-5255-2191-1 (Paperback)
978-1-5255-2192-8 (eBook)

1. JUVENILE FICTION, HUMOROUS STORIES

Distributed to the trade by The Ingram Book Company

CPSIA information can be obtained
at www.ICGtesting.com
Printed in the USA
LVHW07*0316100918
589649LV00016B/73/P

9 781525 521904